Kit and Kaboodle
BLAST OFF TO SPACE

By Michelle Portice
Art by Mitch Mortimer

HIGHLIGHTS PRESS
Honesdale, Pennsylvania

Dear Parents,

Highlights Puzzle Readers are an innovative approach to learning to read that combines puzzles and stories to build motivated, confident readers.

Developed in collaboration with reading experts, the stories and puzzles are seamlessly integrated so that readers are encouraged to read the story, solve the puzzles, and then read the story again. This helps increase vocabulary and reading fluency and creates a satisfying reading experience for any kind of learner. In addition, solving Hidden Pictures puzzles fosters important reading and learning skills such as:

- shape and letter recognition
- letter-sound relationships
- visual discrimination
- logic
- flexible thinking
- sequencing

With high-interest stories, humorous characters, and trademark puzzles, Highlights Puzzle Readers offer a winning combination for inspiring young learners to love reading.

This
is Kit.

This is
Kaboodle.

They love to travel.
You can help them on
each adventure.

As you read the story,
find the objects in each
Hidden Pictures
puzzle.

Then check the
Packing List on
pages 30–31 to make
sure you found everything.

Happy reading!

3

ROCKET

4

Kit and Kaboodle are at space camp.

"What will we do at space camp?"
asks Kaboodle.

"There's lots to do at space camp!"
says Kit. "We will walk on the moon.
We will build a rocket and blast off
into space."

"That's a lot to do in one day," says Kaboodle.

"Yes," says Kit. "We should get ready!"

Kit puts on her flight suit.

"There are too many pockets," she says.

Kaboodle puts on his flight suit.

"There aren't enough pockets," he says.

"We need patches for our suits," says Kit. "What can we use to draw a patch?"

"I packed a few things we can use to draw a cool patch," says Kaboodle.

He looks in his pockets.

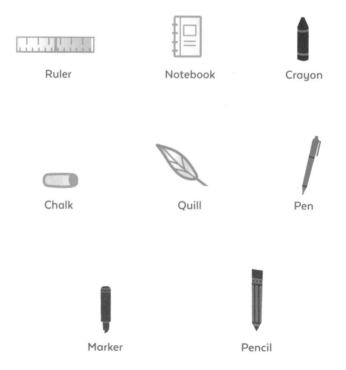

Ruler   Notebook   Crayon

Chalk   Quill   Pen

Marker   Pencil

MERCURY
1958-63

GEMINI
196-

APOLLO
1961-75

9

"I will make my patch a circle," says Kit.

"My patch will be a triangle," says Kaboodle.

"I'm drawing a planet on my patch," says Kit.

"I want to draw a rocket," says Kaboodle.

"Don't forget to add your name!" exclaims Kit.

"Now it's time to walk on the moon," says Kit.

"This special chair will make it feel like we are on the moon," says Kaboodle.

"It will feel like we're floating!" exclaims Kit.

"I packed a few things that can float," says Kaboodle.

He looks in his pockets.

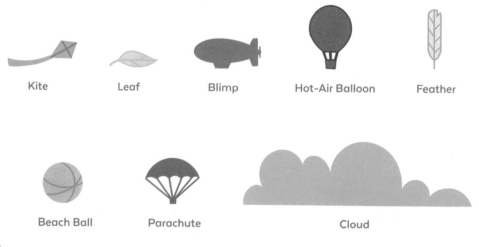

Kite   Leaf   Blimp   Hot-Air Balloon   Feather

Beach Ball   Parachute   Cloud

"Whee!" shouts Kit.
"The moon feels squishy!"

14

"Whee!" exclaims Kaboodle.
"Walking on the moon is fun!"

15

"Now it's time to build a rocket," says Kit. "What can we use to build a rocket?"

"I packed a few things we can use to build a rocket," says Kaboodle.

He looks in his pockets.

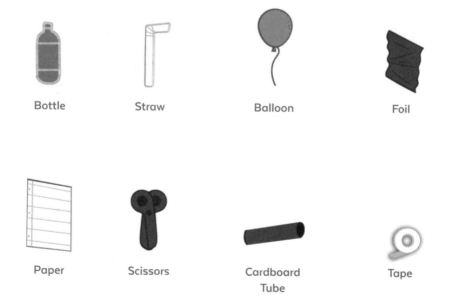

Bottle   Straw   Balloon   Foil

Paper   Scissors   Cardboard Tube   Tape

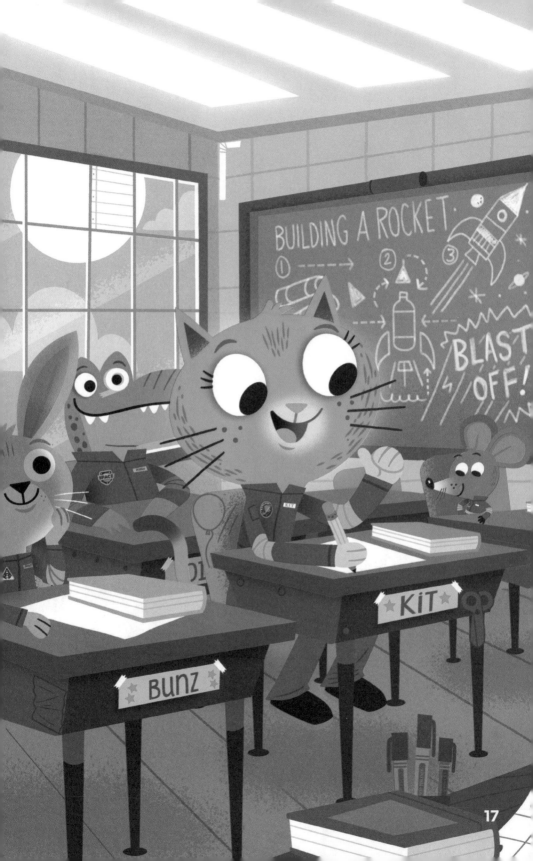

"I wonder how high our rocket will fly," says Kaboodle.

"There's only one way to find out," says Kit. "Let's launch them!"

"Look!" says Kaboodle.

"I see a rocket with pink stars."

"Wow!" says Kit.

"I see a rocket with an orange sun."

"Our rocket flew so high!" says Kaboodle.
"Now it's time to eat lunch."

"I wonder what astronauts eat," says Kit.

"I packed some space food,"
says Kaboodle.

He looks in his pockets.

Hamburger

Apple

French Fries

Slice of Pizza

Sandwich

Carrot

Cookie

Orange

After lunch, Kaboodle goes for a space walk. He helps fix a broken light.

"I fixed the light!" says Kaboodle.

Kit takes a turn in the spinning chair.

She goes backward and forward.

She goes upside down.

"I'm upside down!" says Kit.

"We're done training," says Kaboodle.
"Now we're ready to blast off to space!"

"I'm so excited!" says Kit.
"When do we blast off to space?"

"I packed a few things we can use
to count down to launch," says Kaboodle.

He looks in his pockets.

Stopwatch   Clock   Phone   Timer

Hourglass   Candle   Alarm Clock   Wristwatch

Kit and Kaboodle board the space shuttle.

"Ready?" asks Kit.

"Ready!" says Kaboodle.

"3, 2, 1 . . . We have lift off!" says Kit.

"We made it to space!" says Kaboodle.

Kit and Kaboodle touch down on Earth.
They exit the space shuttle.

"It's nice to be back," says Kaboodle.

"Space camp was a blast!" says Kit.

"Where should we go
on our next trip?" asks Kaboodle.

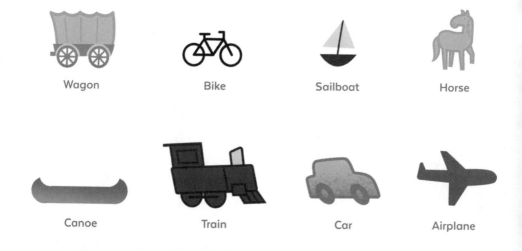

Wagon   Bike   Sailboat   Horse

Canoe   Train   Car   Airplane

Did you find all the things Kit and

Airplane

Alarm Clock

Apple

Balloon

Candle

Canoe

Car

Cardboard Tube

Cookie

Crayon

Feather

Foil

Hourglass

Kite

Leaf

Marker

Pen

Pencil

Phone

Quill

Slice of Pizza

Stopwatch

Straw

Tape

Kaboodle packed for their trip?

 Beach Ball

 Bike

 Blimp

 Bottle

 Carrot

 Chalk

 Clock

 Cloud

 French Fries

 Hamburger

 Horse

 Hot-Air Balloon

 Notebook

 Orange

 Paper

 Parachute

 Ruler

 Sailboat

 Sandwich

 Scissors

 Timer

 Train

 Wagon

 Wristwatch

For information about permission to reprint selections from this book,
please contact permissions@highlights.com.

Published by Highlights Press
815 Church Street
Honesdale, Pennsylvania 18431
ISBN (paperback): 978-1-64472-133-9
ISBN (hardcover): 978-1-64472-134-6
ISBN (ebook): 978-1-64472-241-1

Library of Congress Control Number: 2020934010
Manufactured in Melrose Park, IL, USA
Mfg. 09/2020

First edition
Visit our website at Highlights.com.
10 9 8 7 6 5 4 3 2 1

This book has been officially leveled with both the F&P Text Level
Gradient™ Leveling System and the Lexile® Text Measure.

For assistance in the preparation of this book, the editors would like
to thank Vanessa Maldonado, MSEd, MS Literacy Ed. K–12, Reading/LA
Consultant Cert., K–5 Literacy Instructional Coach; and Gina Shaw.

5